Little Princesses
The Whispering Princess

www.**kidsatrandomhouse**.co.uk/littleprincesses

Little Princesses
The Whispering Princess

By Katie Chase

Illustrated by Leighton Noyes

Red Fox

Special thanks to Narinder Dhami

THE WHISPERING PRINCESS
A RED FOX BOOK 978 0 099 48828 6 (from January 2007)
0 099 48828 0

First published in Great Britain by Red Fox,
an imprint of Random House Children's Books

This edition published 2006

1 3 5 7 9 10 8 6 4 2

Series created by Working Partners Ltd
Copyright © Working Partners Ltd, 2006
Illustrations copyright © Leighton Noyes, 2006
Cover illustration by Nila Aye

Papers used by Random House Children's Books are natural, recyclable products
made from wood grown in sustainable forests. The manufacturing processes conform
to the environmental regulations of the country of origin.

Set in 15/21pt Bembo Schoolbook

Red Fox Books are published by Random House Children's Books,
61–63 Uxbridge Road, London W5 5SA,
a division of The Random House Group Ltd,
in Australia by Random House Australia (Pty) Ltd,
20 Alfred Street, Milsons Point, Sydney, NSW 2061, Australia,
in New Zealand by Random House New Zealand Ltd,
18 Poland Road, Glenfield, Auckland 10, New Zealand,
and in South Africa by Random House (Pty) Ltd,
Isle of Houghton, Corner Boundary Road & Carse O'Gowrie,
Houghton 2198, South Africa

THE RANDOM HOUSE GROUP Limited Reg. No. 954009
www.kidsatrandomhouse.co.uk

A CIP catalogue record for this book is available from the British Library.

Printed and bound in Great Britain by Cox & Wyman Ltd, Reading, Berkshire

For Alice Buchanan

Chapter One

"I can't *wait* to see the castle!" Rosie exclaimed, pressing her nose against the car window to stare out at the Scottish Highlands as the countryside zipped past. The mountains were purple with heather, their peaks wreathed in curling mist; they looked magical.

"I wonder if Great-aunt Rosamund has decorated the Great Hall?" Rosie continued thoughtfully. "She said she might. It'll be cold now it's autumn, so we'll have to light the fire in there every evening. It will be just like

medieval times with
the flames leaping
and crackling. And
I'll be just like a
real princess!"

Rosie's mum turned round
in the passenger seat. "You'll have
to start behaving like a real princess
from now on, then," she said, smiling.

"Well, Great-aunt Rosamund *does*
call me her Little Princess,"

Rosie reminded her. "Although I don't think princesses have hair like mine," she sighed, as she tried to smooth down her wild, reddish-brown curls.

"Does that mean I'll be a prince?" asked Rosie's five-year-old brother, Luke, pulling a face. "I'd rather be a footballer."

"You're just a pest!" Rosie laughed, grabbing Luke and tickling him.

"Stop it!" Luke squawked, wriggling in his seat. He grabbed a handful of Rosie's long curls and tugged.

"Ow!" Rosie squealed, and released her brother.

Luke peered out of the window. "Dad, are we nearly there yet?" he asked impatiently.

Mr Campbell rolled his eyes. "If I had a pound for every time you've asked that question, I'd never have to work again!"

"*Really?*" Luke asked, his blue eyes wide, while Rosie laughed.

"Isn't it just like Rosamund to go off travelling the world at the drop of a hat?" Mr Campbell remarked admiringly. "She's the most adventurous person I know."

Rosie nodded in agreement. Bright and breezy, adventurous and fun, Great-aunt Rosamund, with her floaty scarves, jingling bracelets and long, flowing skirts,

was Rosie's favourite relative. For the last
three summers she had been to stay with her
great-aunt, and there was never a dull
moment. The last time had been on Rosie's
ninth birthday, a few months ago. They had
ridden on horseback across the hills, sailed on
the icy waters of the loch and picnicked in
the heather, watching the birds and the deer
with binoculars. But best of all were the
magical stories her great-aunt told as they
sat snugly by the roaring fire in the Great
Hall every evening.

"A story's not a story unless it's full of
magic and mystery!" Great-aunt Rosamund
always said.

Rosie grinned to herself. She knew her
great-aunt had inherited the old Scottish
castle, along with many of the antiques that
filled the rooms, from her eccentric father.

A collector and explorer, he had gathered weird and wonderful objects from all over the world. And Rosamund had followed in his footsteps. Now she was away for two years, travelling and collecting more antiques, while Rosie and her family moved in to look after the castle.

Rosie had found it hard to leave her old school and say goodbye to her friends. But she couldn't really be sad when she was going to live in a *castle*! It wouldn't be *quite* the same without Great-aunt Rosamund. But it would be exciting to have her friends from home to stay.

"Are we nearly there *now*, Dad?" Luke demanded. Mr Campbell just groaned.

"I wonder what my new school will be like," Rosie said, suddenly feeling a bit nervous.

"Rosamund says it's lovely," replied Mrs Campbell. "And I'm sure you'll soon make new friends."

Rosie nodded. Anyway, she had the whole of half-term to look forward to before she started at her new school.

"Guess what, Luke?" Mr Campbell said as he turned the car into a long gravel drive. "We're here!"

Rosie held her breath, waiting for that first, magical glimpse of her great-aunt's home. And, suddenly, the car rounded a bend in the drive and there it was . . .

The grey stone castle rose majestically into the air, towering against the blue sky. It had one large round tower and four smaller turrets with arched windows, just like a castle in a storybook. Beside it, the calm waters of the loch shimmered in the sunshine.

"Cool!" Luke exclaimed in awe. It was the first time he'd seen the castle since he was a baby.

"It's just as perfect as I remember," Rosie said approvingly, climbing out of the car.

Luke followed her excitedly, his trainers crunching on the gravel. "I can play Robin Hood!" he declared happily. "I'm going to run right round the castle, and see how long it takes." And he disappeared round the side of the building.

Mr Campbell opened the boot to unload the suitcases, while Mrs Campbell took out a

big, old-fashioned key
and turned it in the
enormous iron lock.

Rosie pushed the heavy oak
door open and hurried inside.
She found herself standing in the
Great Hall, with its wide stone fireplace
and two comfy sofas piled with colourful
cushions. She looked around eagerly. The hall
was full of beautiful antiques that Great-aunt
Rosamund or her father had collected on
their travels. There were painted vases, an oak
dresser stacked with blue and white china, a
huge, fringed Persian
rug, and cupboards
and tables all
crammed with
leather-bound
books, silver photo

frames, decorative plates and coloured glass-
ware. Medieval tapestries lined the walls.

Rosie noticed a wooden chest in one
corner that hadn't been there last time she
visited. And a huge mirror on the wall was
new too. She wandered around the room,
staring curiously at other objects she hadn't
seen before: a collection of tropical,
creamy-coloured shells, a porcelain
tea-set of red and blue
and gold, and a
huge fan
painted with
Japanese
figures. She
beamed happily.
It was great to be back!

Rosie went outside to help
her mum and dad unload the car.

As she stepped out of the front door Luke came charging round the other side of the castle.

"I ran all the way round!" he panted.

Rosie grabbed his arm as he dashed past. "Come on, let's get your toys out of the car," she suggested.

"Where *are* my toys?" Luke asked, sticking his head into the car, and pulling out boxes and bags. "I can't find them."

Rosie rolled her eyes. "They're in the boxes marked *Luke's toys!*" she said, pointing them out. "Mum, can I have the room I had last time?"

"Of course," her mum laughed. "Take some of your stuff with you, but leave anything heavy for your dad and me."

Rosie grabbed her rucksack and hurried up the steep, winding staircase that led to a

little round room at
the top of one of the
castle's four turrets –
her bedroom.

She opened the
door and gazed
happily at the familiar
room. It had been
Great-aunt
Rosamund's
bedroom when she
was a little girl and
Rosie loved the
way the wooden
furniture had
been built to
curve neatly
round the walls. The
ceiling was brightly

painted with birds and butterflies among fluffy white clouds, and the tall, arched windows looked right out over the gleaming waters of the loch.

Suddenly, Rosie noticed a note pinned to the plump white pillow on the old wooden bed. I bet it's from Great-aunt Rosamund! she thought excitedly. She snatched up the piece of paper and unfolded it. The note said,

My Little Princess,

I hope you will be very happy in my castle (or should I say your castle) for the next few years. Lots of adventures await you! Expect the unexpected and always be on the lookout for secrets and treasures. But most importantly, read this letter again when you are sitting by the fire tonight!

Lots of love,

Great-aunt Rosamund

Rosie felt a thrill of excitement. What was Great-aunt Rosamund up to? she wondered. And why did she have to read the letter again tonight? One thing was for sure though, she would definitely do as the note said because, knowing her great-aunt, something interesting was bound to happen!

"Rosie!"

Rosie heard Luke calling her, and looked up in time to see him appear at the top of the winding stone steps.

"Can I have a look at your bedroom?" he asked, racing through the door without waiting for an answer, his face red with excitement and his blond hair sticking up in tufts.

"Wow!" he exclaimed, running around the room like an athlete on a track. "This is great! I hope I get a round room too."

Rosie laughed. "I think there's another

bedroom in one of the other turrets. Let's go and look," she said.

They went out into the corridor, just as Mr Campbell appeared at the top of the stairs, heaving a large suitcase.

"Did you bring a ton of bricks with you, by any chance, Rosie?" he enquired, panting.

Rosie grinned, and shook her head. Then she and Luke hurried down the staircase. Rosie carefully slipped her great-aunt's letter into her pocket as she went. She could hardly wait until the evening.

There was so much to do that Rosie was busy all afternoon. It took her ages to put her clothes away and cram all her books and games into the curved cupboards. Luke decided to come and help her – which meant that things took twice as long – but he soon disappeared when their mum called to say that dinner was ready.

When Rosie got downstairs her dad was kneeling in front of the hearth in the Great Hall, lighting the fire.

"That's lovely, Dad," Rosie said, holding her hands out to the crackling flames. The castle was icy cold now that night had fallen. Luckily there were fireplaces in all the rooms.

"Come on," her dad said, getting to his feet. "I don't know about you, but I'm starving."

"Me too," Rosie agreed. She sniffed the air. "And I can smell my favourite – spaghetti bolognese!"

Although the castle kitchen, with its old pine cupboards and stone floor, was enormous, it was kept warm and cosy by the huge Aga in the corner. Luke was already sitting at the scrubbed pine table with a big plate of spaghetti in front of him.

"Leave some for me, greedy guts!" Rosie teased, slipping into the seat next to him.

By the time dinner was over, Luke was trying not to yawn.

"Time for bed, Luke," Dad said, as he helped Mrs Campbell collect the dirty plates.

"Oh, do I *have* to?" Luke groaned.

"Yes," his mum replied firmly.

Mr Campbell heaved Luke out of his chair, sat him on his shoulders and marched him off to bed.

Mrs Campbell laughed. "I'd better put the last few things away in Luke's room," she said, hurrying after her husband.

As her parents and Luke disappeared upstairs, Rosie wandered into the Great Hall. The fire was blazing now, the flames casting flickering shadows on the walls. Rosie walked around the room for a while, looking at some of her great-aunt's treasures. Then she curled up comfortably in a corner of one of the plump sofas by the fire.

As Rosie wriggled slightly, trying to get comfy amidst the cushions, she heard the faint crackle of paper in her pocket. Straight away she sat up, brimming with excitement.

In all the hustle and bustle, she'd almost
forgotten about her great-aunt's note! And
now here she was, in front of the fire, just as
the letter had said. It was time to read it
again . . .

Rosie pulled the note out of her pocket
and scanned it eagerly. She felt a bit
disappointed when nothing happened, even
though she didn't *quite* know what she had
been expecting.

But then, as she leaned forward to stare at
the letter more closely in the firelight, Rosie
blinked and blinked again. Was she seeing
things?

She wasn't! As Rosie watched, more of her
great-aunt's writing began to appear, as if by
magic, between the lines of the note.

Chapter Two

Rosie's heart beat faster. She was looking at a secret message from her great-aunt!

At first the writing was very pale and faint, and Rosie couldn't read it. But as she leaned closer to the fire the heat from the flames seemed to make the words darker. Rosie guessed that her great-aunt had used some kind of special invisible ink. But what did the message say?

Look for the little princesses around the castle and when you find one always remember to curtsey and say "Hello"! Rosie read.

What did the message mean? she wondered. And who were these "little princesses" around the castle? Where could they be?

Shaking with excitement, Rosie jumped to her feet. She was about to start searching for a little princess but at that moment her mum came into the Great Hall.

"I think you should be off to bed now, Rosie," she said with a yawn. "You must be exhausted. I know I am."

"Oh, *Mum*!" Rosie groaned. Now that she knew about the little princesses, she thought she'd *burst* if she didn't get the chance to look around. "I'm not a bit tired. Please can I stay up a little while longer?"

"No, it's almost nine o'clock, and we've had a long day," her mum said firmly, shooing Rosie out of the hall. "If you're quick, you can read for a few minutes before you go to sleep."

Rosie nodded and ran up the staircase to her room. At least I'll be able to search my bedroom, she thought. She raced in through the door and looked around, half-expecting a little princess to pop out from somewhere and shout, *Here I am!* But nothing happened.

Quickly Rosie put on her pyjamas, staring around the room as she did so. There were tapestries on the walls but they showed forest scenes with animals and no little princesses at all. As she cleaned her teeth at the basin she examined the big oak wardrobe. The doors were carved with animals and flowers but, again, there was nothing that looked anything like a princess.

But Rosie wouldn't give up. She dashed around the room, peering into every nook and cranny for a little princess but she found nothing. Then she heard her mum coming up the stairs and quickly jumped into bed.

"Oh, good, you're in bed already," Mrs Campbell said as she came in. "I think Luke's managed to calm down and get to sleep at last! Goodnight, sweetheart." She bent over and gave Rosie a kiss. "Now, remember, lights out in five minutes."

"OK," Rosie agreed.

Mrs Campbell went downstairs and Rosie lay back against the pillows, staring up at the painted ceiling above her.

"Maybe it's like a puzzle in one of my puzzle books," Rosie said to herself. "Maybe the little princess is really well hidden and it takes ages to find her."

So Rosie gazed at the ceiling until she almost went cross-eyed. But, despite her

efforts, all she could see were pretty bluebirds and pink butterflies fluttering among the billowing white clouds. That meant she'd have to wait till tomorrow, when she could search the rest of the castle.

"I bet I don't sleep a *wink*," Rosie muttered, leaning over to turn off her bedside lamp. "How *can* I when I know something magical is going on?"

But, just as her fingers touched the light switch, Rosie drew her hand back abruptly, almost tumbling out of bed with excitement. The one thing in the whole room she hadn't taken a good look at was the beautiful Persian rug that lay right beside her bed.

Rosie bobbed up from under the duvet
and leaned over the edge of the bed to get
a better look. The rug was old, but its jewel-
bright colours glowed in the lamplight. It was
fringed with yellow and blue thread and in

the middle was a large picture. The background was a rolling desert of golden sand dunes with a vast, snowy mountain towering over the landscape in the distance. On top of the mountain sat a golden lamp. Rosie was intrigued to see that the lamp was open, and a plume of white smoke seemed to be drifting from it.

"It's just like Aladdin's lamp!" Rosie said to herself.

Her gaze moved to the middle of the picture, where there stood a city of white buildings with round domes and minarets, surrounded by mosaic pavements. In the very centre was an ornate white palace with an exotic garden full of fountains and trees and flowers. Above the palace Rosie saw a flying carpet speeding along on the breeze. And upon the carpet, her legs crossed and her big brown eyes sad and forlorn, sat a beautiful girl dressed in rich silken clothes.

"A little princess!" Rosie gasped, getting tangled up in her duvet as she tried to jump out of bed too fast. "It must be!"

She fought her way out of the duvet and stood next to the rug, her heart pounding with excitement. Then she bobbed down into her best curtsey, just as Great-aunt Rosamund had told her.

"Hello!" Rosie whispered breathlessly, staring right into the little princess's eyes.

As soon as she had spoken Rosie felt a soft, scented breeze swirl up from the centre of the rug. The breeze was very warm and Rosie saw that it held grains of glittering golden sand. It wrapped itself around her, making her hair stream out and filling every corner of the room.

Rosie gasped as the breeze grew stronger, suddenly becoming a powerful whirlwind. Feeling the grains of sand whipping around her face, Rosie put her hands up to protect herself and closed her eyes. As she did so the whirlwind grew faster, the winds whistled in her ears, and then, to her surprise, Rosie felt herself lifted gently off her feet and carried swiftly through the air.

Chapter Three

"Oh!" Rosie exclaimed, as her feet touched the ground and she took her hands away from her face. "This is definitely *not* my bedroom!"

She gazed around in astonishment to see that she was standing in the beautiful garden she had been looking at just a moment before, in the picture on her bedside rug. The garden was even more gorgeous in real life. Lush and colourful, it was full of pink and red hibiscus flowers that mingled with white roses and trailing jasmine. The air was heady

with the perfume
of the flowers and
peacocks strutted here
and there, spreading
their feathery tails out to
the blazing sun overhead.

Nearby, a marble fountain sent water
splashing into an octagonal pond lined with
sparkling blue and green mosaic tiles. The
golden flash of a fish caught Rosie's eye, but
then it had gone, slipping away beneath a
large pink water lily.

"Wow!" Rosie murmured, her eyes wide.
She'd known that Great-aunt Rosamund had
something special in store for her – but this
was spectacular!

"Hello," someone whispered behind her.

Rosie spun round. A pretty girl with long,
raven-black hair and sad brown eyes was

smiling at her. She was richly dressed in
green and blue silk, and she wore a cropped
top and billowing trousers that were decorated with gold thread and glittering jewels.
A dainty gold tiara twinkled on top of her

turban, with one large, green, teardrop-
shaped emerald hanging down onto her
forehead. And on her wrist she wore a
tinkling silver bell, which jingled as she
moved. Rosie recognized her immediately –
it was the girl she had seen in the picture
on the rug.

"You're the little princess from my rug!"
Rosie exclaimed. "But where am I?"

The girl looked puzzled. "Don't you
know?" she breathed. "We're in the palace
garden."

"But *where*?" asked Rosie. As she looked
around she caught sight of her own clothes
and realized that her pink pyjamas had
somehow disappeared. Now she was wearing
a lilac silk outfit, with a cropped top and
baggy trousers, just like the little princess
herself.

"In Persia," the girl whispered, looking even more puzzled.

Rosie was astonished. Persia? Surely that was an ancient country from long ago? She remembered Great-aunt Rosamund mentioning it in one of her stories.

"I'm Princess Azara," the girl went on in her whispery voice. "I'm really glad to see you, but how did you get here?"

Rosie laughed. "I don't *know* how I got here," she replied. "You see, my name's Rosie and my Great-aunt Rosamund told me to find all the little princesses in her castle—"

"Rosamund?" Azara interrupted softly, looking excited. "Did you say *Rosamund*?"

Rosie nodded, wondering why Azara whispered all the time. She decided that perhaps the little princess was ill and had a sore throat.

"My grandmother used to tell me stories about when she was a little girl," Azara explained, so quietly Rosie had to lean closer to hear the words. "She told me a girl called Rosamund used to come and visit her, and they had all sorts of adventures together. That would have been about fifty years ago."

"That must have been *my* Great-aunt Rosamund!" gasped Rosie. "So she came here too, just like me?"

Azara nodded. "My grandmother and your Great-aunt Rosamund worked out that she'd come from the future," she went on in a whisper. "My grandmother said that Rosamund called our country Ancient Persia – although it doesn't feel ancient to us!"

Rosie could hardly believe her ears. This really *was* magic!

"But your great-aunt stopped visiting after

a time," Azara sighed. "I suppose the magic that brought her here doesn't work when people grow up."

"But now *I'm* here!" replied Rosie, taking Azara's hand. "Maybe we could be friends too, just like Great-aunt Rosamund and your grandmother?"

"I'd like that," Azara breathed, looking more cheerful, even though she seemed to find it very difficult to speak. "I don't have any friends."

"Is that why you look so sad?" Rosie asked sympathetically. "I thought it might be because you don't feel well."

"You mean because I'm whispering?"

sighed Azara. "I'm not sick, I just can't help it. Abdul the evil genie has put a spell on me."

"Oh, no!" Rosie gasped. She led Azara over to a marble seat among the flowers. "Let's sit down, and you can tell me all about it."

Azara looked very downhearted. "Abdul tricked someone into letting him out of his lamp," she whispered. "Then he imprisoned my father in the palace dungeons and took over the kingdom! Everyone in the city hates him because he's mean and selfish and flies into the most terrible rages."

"But why did he take your voice away?" asked Rosie.

"Because I'm the only person who knows the song to make the magic carpet fly," Azara explained, very quietly. "My grandmother taught it to me when I was little. But she died a year ago, and now I'm the only person who knows the song. The genie's very vain – he doesn't want anyone else in the kingdom to be able to work magic like him. And without my voice I can hardly speak, let alone sing the magic words."

"He sounds horrible," Rosie declared indignantly.

"He is," hissed Azara. "He keeps my voice in a little bottle which he wears on a red string round his neck, so I have no way of getting it. And just to make sure" – she held up her wrist and the silver bell she wore jingled loudly – "Abdul makes me wear this bell so that he always knows where I am. He's put a very powerful spell on it so I can't take it off."

Rosie frowned. "Surely there must be a way to get rid of him?" she asked.

Azara sighed. "The only way to defeat him is to return him to his lamp," she whispered. "But no one knows where he's hidden it. If I had my voice," she went on sadly, "I would take the magic carpet and fly off to look for it. But without my voice I can't sing to make the carpet fly."

Rosie patted her arm reassuringly. "Well there's one thing you *can* do," she said firmly. "You can try to get your voice back. And I'm going to help you!"

Chapter Four

"Oh, that would be wonderful!" Azara gasped, clapping her hands with joy. But as she did so the bell on her wrist jingled loudly. Azara's face fell. "But it's impossible because of *this*!" she whispered, pointing at the bell. "I've tried to get my voice back before, when the genie was asleep. But the bell always wakes him before I can get close enough to untie the string and get the bottle."

"Yes, but *I'm* not wearing a bell, am I?" Rosie laughed, holding up her wrists.

"We'll wait until Abdul's fast asleep, and

then *I'll* take the bottle."

Azara looked thrilled. "Thank you, Rosie," she breathed gratefully. "No one else will help me. All the palace servants are too scared of Abdul."

"Well, he doesn't scare me!" Rosie replied in a determined voice.

"I AM THE BEST, THE MOST POWERFUL, THE MOST MAGICAL GENIE IN THE WHOLE WIDE WORLD!" roared somebody from inside the palace.

Rosie almost jumped out of her skin. "Is that . . . Is that *him*?" she asked nervously.

Azara nodded. "He's always in a bad mood," she hissed.

"Let's go and see what's upset him," suggested Rosie bravely. "If we're going to get your voice back, I'd better take a look at Abdul so we can decide on a plan."

★ 41 ★

Azara nodded and got up to lead the way. "But you must be careful, Rosie," she whispered. "Abdul's magic is very powerful."

Rosie followed Azara into the palace and down a white marble corridor lined with beautiful wall paintings. As they drew nearer to the throne room she could hear Abdul complaining.

"That idiot, Jabbar! He says he's a more powerful genie than me, does he? What nonsense! He may have escaped from his magic ring but I'll soon turn him into a frog or a snake!" the genie cried.

"Abdul hates the Genie of the Ring, Jabbar," Azara whispered to Rosie. "He doesn't like anyone else to have magic powers."

They had reached a pair of tall golden doors. One of them stood slightly ajar;

Rosie and Azara peeped inside.

The throne room was
dazzling with its white
marble columns and blue
and gold mosaic floor. The
golden throne itself stood
on a marble platform
at one end of the
chamber; it was
carved in the shape
of a peacock's tail.
Abdul was stomping
up and down the room,
biting his lip and
sulking. He was
tall and broad-
shouldered, and he wore
rich, red silk robes. Rosie saw that
his skin was a dark bottle-green, and his eyes

were deep holes that burned and flashed with flames of fire.

"I *am* the most powerful genie in the world, *aren't* I?" he shouted at two servants who were cowering in the corner.

"Of course you are, master," they said quickly, looking petrified.

"What do you know about magic?" Abdul roared, taking an orange from the fruit bowl and hurling it at them. "Get out, fools!"

Abdul pointed his finger at the servants who were now running from the hall. Fiery red sparks jumped and crackled around his hand, and then a bolt of jagged red fire suddenly shot out and hit one of the servants in the back. Immediately he turned into a big, round orange and rolled across the floor!

"I see what you mean. That genie is very

bad-tempered," Rosie murmured to Azara as the other servant ran out into the corridor. She looked more closely at Abdul and saw the red string he wore round his neck. A tiny silver bottle hung from it.

"Don't go in there, Your Highness," the servant said shakily to Azara. "He's in a terrible mood today."

"Fetch the court musicians," Azara whispered to the servant. "Maybe they will be able to calm him." She turned to Rosie. "Abdul likes music," she explained softly. "Sometimes he falls asleep when the musicians play."

Rosie nodded, hoping the music would lull Abdul to sleep. She was determined to help Azara get her voice back, even though the genie was very scary indeed.

"What's all that whispering about?" Abdul suddenly shouted crossly from the throne room. "And who are *you*?" he demanded, spotting Rosie for the first time.

"This is my friend, Rosie, o Magical One," Azara croaked as loudly as she could.

Rosie tried not to shiver as the genie's burning eyes met hers.

"Can you amuse me, girl?" Abdul snapped. "Can you dance? Can you sing?" He frowned, his great black eyebrows

nearly meeting in the middle so that he looked even more frightening. "Can you do any *magic tricks*?" he thundered.

"Oh, no, Your Magicalness," Rosie said quickly. "I can't do *any* magic tricks at all." The genie looked extremely pleased at this. Just at that moment the musicians came running into the room, carrying their instruments and looking very frightened.

"Play something soft and sweet," Azara whispered to them, carefully picking up the orange that had once been a servant and moving it out of harm's way.

The musicians hurried forwards.

"Get on with it!" Abdul shouted grumpily.

Rosie and Azara backed quietly out of the doors as the musicians began to play. The soft, tuneful sounds of the flutes and harps floated around the room, filling the air.

"Hmmm, that's better," Abdul grunted. He slumped down on the golden throne, still looking rather annoyed. But, after five minutes or so, Rosie and Azara peeped into the room to see that the genie was beginning to look much more relaxed.

Rosie's heart began to beat faster as she saw the genie's eyelids droop. The next moment he was snoring gently. "He's asleep," Rosie hissed. "I'm going to try and get the bottle."

At a sign from Azara the musicians left the

throne room on tiptoe. Abdul didn't stir.

"Please be careful, Rosie," Azara whispered anxiously.

Rosie nodded. She slipped through the golden doors and crept across the floor towards the throne. Still Abdul didn't move.

Rosie climbed the steps to the throne and paused. She was so close to the genie now that she could reach out and touch him.

And there was the tiny silver bottle on its cord round his neck.

Rosie tiptoed behind the genie and gently began to untie the knot in the red string. But then Abdul stirred and yawned loudly. Rosie froze. The genie seemed to be waking up.

Chapter Five

Rosie was so nervous she couldn't have
moved even if she'd wanted to. She stayed
exactly where she was, holding her breath
and praying that Abdul wouldn't wake up
and realize what she was doing. She could
see Azara peering round the door, looking
extremely frightened.

But after a few, very long moments Abdul
sank back down on the throne and began to
snore.

Thank goodness, Rosie thought. She
untied the string with trembling fingers, and

carefully lifted the bottle from around the genie's neck. Then she slipped back to join Azara as quickly as she could.

"Oh, Rosie, that was close!" Azara gasped.

"I know," Rosie agreed. "Here's your voice back." And she handed Azara the little silver bottle.

Beaming all over her face, Azara opened the bottle and lifted it to her lips. Rosie watched curiously as a thin, silvery stream of shimmering mist drifted out of the bottle, curled into Azara's mouth and disappeared from view.

But before Azara could speak there was a loud roar

from inside the throne room.

"GUARDS! I'VE BEEN ROBBED! FIND THE THIEF!"

"Oh, no!" Azara cried. "Abdul's awake, and he's noticed that the bottle has gone!" Then she touched her throat, looking delighted. "My voice! It's back!"

"That's great, Azara," Rosie said breathlessly, as she heard the sound of angry footsteps thumping across the throne room. "But maybe we should get out of here."

"Follow me," Azara said.

She ran down the corridor and whisked aside a silk curtain, to reveal a door. The girls dashed through it into a small courtyard with a tinkling silver fountain. Behind them they could hear the sound of shouting and more footsteps, as guards ran to the throne room.

Azara grabbed Rosie's hand and pulled her out of the courtyard, along a maze of white marble corridors, through archways and up a broad, twisting staircase.

When Rosie was so out of breath she thought she couldn't run any more, Azara flung open a silver door. "This is my bed-chamber," she explained, ushering Rosie inside and closing the door.

Rosie gasped in wonder as she stared around the room. It really *was* fit for a little princess. A large, circular silver bed stood in the centre of the room, draped with a canopy of lilac silk curtains. Violet and silver satin cushions, embroidered with jewels, were scattered across the pillows and a tall silver mirror, studded with sparkling gems, stood near the far wall. Four huge, arched win-dows, each with an elaborately carved white

marble balcony, looked out over the beautiful
palace gardens.

As Rosie stared around her, she realized
she could hear a strange whistling sound, as
if a strong wind was rushing down the
corridor towards her. "What's that noise?"
Rosie asked.

"It's Abdul!" Azara cried. "He's coming after us!"

"Oh!" Rosie glanced over her shoulder at the door. The noise was getting louder.

"Rosie, quick!" Azara called, dashing across her room to sit cross-legged on the rug beside her bed. "We have to get out of here and find Abdul's lamp. It's the only way to get rid of him."

"But how are we going to get out of the palace?" Rosie began, hurrying over to Azara. Then she looked more closely at the rug Azara was sitting on. It was the flying carpet which had been pictured on the rug in *her* bedroom, back at the castle!

Rosie jumped onto the rug and sat down next to Azara. As she did so the door burst open.

Abdul flew into the room, his face purple

with fury and his eyes blazing with fiery rage. "You can't get away!" he roared as he saw Rosie and Azara sitting on the flying carpet. "My magic will stop you!" He raised his hand, and Rosie saw fierce red sparks crackling and spitting around it.

Chapter Six

Rosie had never felt so scared in her life. She wondered if she and Azara were about to be turned into oranges – or something worse! "What are we going to do?" she gasped as the genie bore down on them.

Azara didn't answer. Instead she began to sing a strange, haunting song: "*Aman amar, arak kiri!*"

The rug immediately rose into the air, leaving a trail of magical golden sparks behind it.

But at that moment Abdul sent a bolt of

red fire shooting across
the room towards
them. Rosie and
Azara both
managed to
dodge the red
lightning bolt just in
time. But Rosie was
caught off balance. She
wobbled and tumbled
over the edge of the flying
carpet, plunging towards the
floor below!

Rosie just managed to grab
one of the carpet's tassels as she fell. But
almost immediately she felt the
silky threads slipping through her fingers.
"Help!" she cried in panic.

Azara threw herself forwards on the carpet

and caught Rosie's hands just as the tassel finally slid from Rosie's grasp. "*Kirit, kandorah!*" Azara sang. At that, the rug zoomed out of the nearest window with Azara still keeping a tight hold on Rosie.

"Come back!" Abdul roared, magically sprouting wings and shooting into the air towards the carpet. "You don't get away from me that easily!" Furiously, he made a grab for Rosie's legs, but missed.

Azara sung a few more commands and the carpet picked up speed and shot away, leaving the genie grabbing uselessly at the trail of magic sparkles.

"Thanks!" Rosie

gasped, as Azara hauled her up onto the carpet. She looked back towards the palace. "Won't Abdul follow us?"

Azara laughed. "He is very powerful," she said. "But even *he* can't fly as fast as the magic carpet!"

"Good!" Rosie said with relief.

The carpet was now zooming over the palace garden. Rosie peered cautiously over the edge and saw climbing roses and scented jasmine spilling over the walls.

"Now," Azara said with a frown, "I wonder where we should start looking for Abdul's lamp?"

But Rosie wasn't really listening. She was looking around thoughtfully, because everything looked very familiar. She could see a city of white buildings surrounding the palace. I've seen all this before, Rosie thought excitedly. In the Persian rug on my bedroom floor!

Rosie frowned in concentration, trying to recall the picture on the rug. There had been a desert and a mountain too, she remembered. And on top of that mountain there had been a golden lamp!

"Azara," Rosie gasped, "I think I know where Abdul's lamp is! I saw it on my Persian rug back home!"

Azara looked thrilled. "Where?" she asked eagerly.

"Is there a big, snow-covered mountain in your land?" Rosie asked.

"Yes, look over there, to the east," Azara replied.

Rosie looked in the direction Azara was pointing. Beyond the city she saw a rolling desert of golden sand. And there, in the far distance, she could see a vast mountain with a snow-covered peak. The same mountain she had seen in the picture on the rug.

Rosie turned to Azara. "I think the lamp is hidden on that mountain top," she explained. "Can the rug take us there?"

"Of course!" Azara exclaimed, her face glowing with excitement.

She sang a few instructions to the flying carpet. "*Amar aman. Karesh!*" Immediately, the carpet changed direction and flew towards the mountain.

Rosie gazed at the ground below as they soared over the desert. She saw green oases dotted here and there, with little pools of sparkling blue water and tall palm trees. She even spotted a camel caravan, making its way slowly through the desert dunes.

The sun began to set, streaking the sky with pink and gold, and still the carpet flew on.

"The mountain is a long way from the city," Azara explained. "But we're getting close now."

The mountain loomed ahead of them as the sky began to darken. Rosie watched in delight as the inky darkness gradually filled with tiny, sparkling stars, like diamonds nestled in a black velvet box.

The carpet hovered over the mountain top and then began to float slowly towards the snowy ground. Rosie and Azara waited impatiently for it to land and then they both jumped off. Their feet sank into thick, soft snow.

"Brr, it's cold!" Azara gasped. "We must find the lamp quickly before we freeze!"

Shivering, Rosie and Azara began to search around the snowy rocks on the mountain top. The moon shone down, making the ice glitter in the pale light, but the girls couldn't see anything in the snow except their own footprints as they searched here and there.

Panting, Rosie waded through the deep snow and scrambled over rocks to reach the

highest part of the mountain. She looked
carefully all around her but there was no sign
of a lamp. She began to wonder if she'd
made a mistake.

She sighed and turned back towards Azara,
but then she stopped. Was she imagining it, or
had she just seen the faintest glimmer of gold
in the snow?

Rosie hurried over to the spot and plunged her fingers into the icy powder. Although her hands were nearly numb with cold, she was sure she could feel something smooth and solid. Excitedly, Rosie brushed the snow away, and there, gleaming in the moonlight, lay Abdul the Genie's golden lamp.

Chapter Seven

"Azara, I've found it!" Rosie called triumphantly, picking up the lamp carefully. It was just about the size of a pencil case.

"That's wonderful!" Azara cried, rushing over to take the lamp. "Thank you so much, Rosie. I'd never have known where to look, without you."

"L–Let's get out of here, now. It's f–f–freezing," Rosie stammered.

Azara tucked the lamp safely into her pocket and the girls rushed back to the magic carpet. They hopped on and, as Azara

began to sing, it rose up into the air again.
This time Rosie held on tightly. The carpet
shot away from the snowy mountain, leaving
a trail of magic sparks that lit up the dark
sky like fireworks.

"It's wonderful that we have the lamp,"
Azara said breathlessly. "But now we have
another problem." She frowned. "How are we
going to get Abdul back *inside* it?"

Rosie looked thoughtful. "I suppose we
can't *make* him go inside?" she asked.

"No," Azara replied, shaking her head.

"And he won't *want* to go back in, because then he's trapped until someone rubs the lamp and releases him again."

"Don't worry," Rosie said firmly. "I'm sure we can think of something."

Both girls fell into a thoughtful silence.

"If we're going to get Abdul back into his lamp, we have to trick him into making himself small," Azara said later, as the flying carpet was soaring over the city once more. "But how can we do that?"

"I think I've got an idea," Rosie replied.

"Just go along with everything I say, however strange it may seem!"

"Very well," Azara agreed.

The carpet flew gracefully through the window into Azara's bedchamber and landed on the floor by her bed. Before the girls could say or do anything, there was an enormous

Bang!

A huge cloud of glittering red smoke exploded in the air, making both girls cough and splutter. When the smoke cleared, there stood Abdul the Genie. He looked as if he was about to burst with rage.

"So you're back!" he roared. "Now you will find out how the mighty Abdul punishes those who disobey him!"

Rosie's knees shook with fright. But she knew she had to act quickly to put the first

part of her plan into operation. "Oh, thank goodness you're here!" she cried. "No one but you can save us!"

"Huh?" Abdul frowned, looking suspicious. "What are you talking about?"

"We're in big trouble," Rosie went on breathlessly. "A great and powerful genie – even more powerful than *you* – is on his way to take over the kingdom!"

Abdul's face darkened with fury. "This cannot be true!" he roared. "If that fool, Jabbar—"

"It is not Jabbar, but a much greater genie," Azara put in hurriedly.

"Indeed," Rosie agreed. "This genie has amazing magic powers! He can reach up into the sky and draw lightning bolts from the thunderclouds to use as weapons against his enemies!"

"I can do that," Abdul boasted.

Rosie shook her head. "But the clouds are so high," she pointed out. "You couldn't possibly reach them."

Abdul's face turned purple with fury. "I'll show YOU!" he roared. "Just watch me!"

Rosie and Azara shrank back as the genie began to spin. Round and round he spun, faster and faster, until his flying robes were a shimmering blur of red. Then, suddenly, he began to grow. Still spinning like a top, he shot up into the air towards the ceiling, towering over the girls and growing taller with every second.

"He's going to burst through the roof!" Azara gasped.

But at the last moment Abdul twisted round and shot through the window. He continued to grow until he was so tall they could no longer see his face.

Suddenly there was a loud clap of thunder and the girls covered their ears.

"Look, he's coming back!" Rosie whispered to Azara.

Abdul was slowly shrinking back to his normal size. As he drew his head and shoulders in through the window, he was beaming smugly all over his face. In his hand he held a long, jagged lightning bolt of shining silver. "See?" he boasted. "I reached right inside the biggest thundercloud I could find and pulled out a lightning bolt. I'm just as powerful as that other genie!"

Rosie and Azara looked impressed.

"That's amazing, but can you swim to the deepest part of the ocean and find a giant oyster shell?" Rosie asked.

"What?" Abdul yelled crossly.

"That's what the other genie did," Azara put in. "He uses the shell as a . . . as a . . ."

"Magic shield," Rosie finished quickly.

"Well, I can do that!" Abdul shouted.

"Do you really think so?" Azara asked doubtfully.

Abdul glared at her. "Of course I can!" he snapped. And with a swirl of his silken robes, he disappeared through the window, this time speeding towards the ocean.

The girls waited
nervously, until a few
minutes later Abdul
returned. He was
dripping wet and
there was seaweed in
his hair, but in his
arms he carried a
giant, blue-black
oyster shell with a
creamy mother-of-
pearl lining.

"See? I have my own magic
shield!" Abdul boasted. "I'd like to see
this genie defeat me *now*!"

Rosie and Azara smiled.

"You're certainly a great genie," Rosie
agreed. "But did you know that the other
genie has a secret weapon?"

"What secret weapon?" Abdul yelled furiously. "Tell me immediately!"

"He has a coat woven from the fur of bumblebees," Rosie explained. "And, as everyone knows, bumblebee fur is the most magical thing in the whole world!"

Abdul looked puzzled. "Are you sure?" he muttered.

"Oh, *yes*!" Azara told him. "Everybody knows *that*!"

The genie coughed. "Well, of course I knew that," he said hurriedly. "But do you think I should have such a coat?"

Rosie nodded. "When he's wearing the coat, the other genie cannot be hurt by magic at all!" she explained.

"I see," Abdul said thoughtfully. He clapped his hands. "Servants!" he shouted. "Bring all the beehives from the palace

 79

gardens immediately!"

Rosie and Azara watched as the wooden beehives were brought in one by one and placed around the bedchamber. Soon the room was filled with the soft buzzing of the bees and the sweet smell of honey.

"Now," Abdul said, picking up a pair of Azara's scissors. "I shall have a *much* better coat than that other genie."

He held out his finger and a large bee landed on it. Abdul immediately tried to snip off its fur. But the bee buzzed loudly and flew off before Abdul could cut off even a tiny bit.

"Come back!" he shouted grumpily. But the bee ignored him and buzzed away.

Rosie and Azara tried not to laugh as they watched the angry genie chasing the bees around the room, trying to snip off their fur. Of course, none of the bees would keep still.

"These scissors are too big," Abdul complained, throwing them down in a temper. "I need a tiny pair."

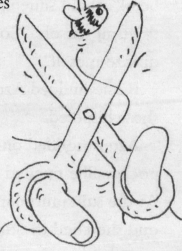

"But then you won't be able to get your fingers through the holes," Rosie pointed out.

"Ha, ha, ha!" Abdul laughed smugly. "That's what *you* think!"

He waved his hand in the air and, with a flash of smoke, he quickly began to shrink. Within seconds he was almost as small as the bee. Then, with another wave of his hand, Abdul shrank the scissors too.

"Now I'll be able to shear those pesky bees!" Abdul squeaked proudly, picking up the tiny scissors. "Sometimes I'm so clever, I amaze myself!"

Rosie nudged Azara. "Now's our chance," she whispered.

Azara nodded and drew the lamp from her pocket. She opened the lid and held it ready. At the same moment Rosie rushed forwards and snatched the tiny genie up in her hand.

"What are you doing?" Abdul squeaked. "Put me down immediately!"

But before he could use any of his magic, Rosie dropped him inside the lamp, and Azara snapped the lid shut.

Chapter Eight

"We did it, Rosie!" Azara cried, her eyes
shining. "Your plan worked!"

There was a muffled bellow from inside the
lamp, which was shaking violently in Azara's
hands. "Let me out! Let me out, I say, or
you'll be sorry!"

"We're not scared of you any more," Rosie
laughed, as courtiers and servants came
crowding into the room to find out what was
going on. Rosie spotted the poor servant that
Abdul had turned into an orange, and
realized with relief that the genie's cruel

magic must have worn off.

"We're free of Abdul at last!" Azara exclaimed, holding the lamp high over her head. "Tell everyone in the city the good news!"

There were loud cheers, and then the servants scattered in all directions to do Azara's bidding. Meanwhile, crowds of happy courtiers escorted Rosie and Azara to the dungeons to release the little princess's father, the sultan.

The dungeons were deep beneath the palace. Rosie followed Azara down a long spiral staircase and then along a low, gloomy passageway. It was dark and stuffy here, for there were none of the beautiful big windows that kept the palace above

so light and airy.

The sultan's cell was very small, with a
heavy wooden door and a tiny window
opening onto the passageway. Two of
the courtiers stepped forwards and drew
back the iron bolts that barred the door.
Then Azara dragged it open and rushed
inside to see her father.

"My beloved child!" the sultan declared in amazement and delight, as all the courtiers bowed low. He looked pale and weary after his long imprisonment and his silk robes were dusty and dirty. But he was beaming all over his face and Rosie watched happily as he hugged his daughter. It made her think about her own family. It really was time she thought about going home.

"Father, it's thanks to my friend Rosie that Abdul is back in his lamp," Azara explained, as everyone made their way back upstairs to the throne room.

The sultan

turned to Rosie. "My dear," he said happily, "we can't thank you enough. You have saved our kingdom!"

The courtiers and servants cheered loudly.

"Abdul will be locked up in the deepest, darkest dungeon in the palace," the sultan went on, pointing at the lamp in Azara's hands "And now, we shall celebrate with a huge party! Everyone in the city is invited!"

He clapped his hands and the servants ran off eagerly to prepare for the celebrations. Meanwhile, Rosie quietly drew Azara to one side.

"I'd love to stay for the party, Azara," Rosie whispered, "but I think I should be going home. I've been gone for ages."

Azara nodded. "Thank you again, Rosie," she said, giving her a hug. "You must come and visit me often, just like your Great-aunt Rosamund visited my grandmother."

"Oh, I will!" Rosie promised, returning the hug warmly. "I'm so glad to have met you, Azara! Goodbye!"

Rosie hadn't been quite sure how she would get home again, but as soon as the word "Goodbye" left her lips she felt a warm breeze whip up around her. Just as before, she was suddenly enveloped in a whirling storm of sparkling golden sand. And, once again, she closed her eyes . . .

The wind died away. Rosie opened her eyes and gazed around. She was back in her turret bedroom at Great-aunt Rosamund's castle. And, strangely, the time on the clock read 9.05 p.m. – only five minutes later than when she had first hopped out of bed to look at her rug!

Yawning, Rosie jumped into bed and switched off her bedside light. But, before she lay down to sleep, she leaned over and smiled at the rug on the floor.

"Goodnight, Azara," she whispered.

Chapter Nine

Still half-asleep, Rosie yawned and rolled
over in bed. She could feel warm sunlight on
her face and she could hear Luke playing
with his toy cars on the spiral staircase
outside her room. Surely it couldn't be
morning already?

Rosie opened her eyes and yawned again.
Now she remembered! She'd had a strange
and magical adventure last night with
Princess Azara. Or had she?

Rosie frowned. She remembered how she
and Azara had defeated Abdul the Genie and

trapped him safely in his lamp, but for a
moment she wasn't quite sure whether it had
all been a dream or not. But then there was
the note with its message in invisible
ink from Great-aunt Rosamund
– or had she dreamed that
too? Rosie couldn't be sure.

The door opened, and
Rosie's mum came in.
"Good morning,
sleepyhead," she
said with a smile.
"Luke's been up
for hours
already."
Then she
came to a
stop in the
middle of

the room. "Goodness, wherever did all this sand come from?"

Rosie immediately sat up and scrambled to the edge of the bed. "What sand?" she asked excitedly.

"It's all over the floor," Mrs Campbell replied, pointing out the grains of golden sand glittering on the flagstones. "I suppose it must have dropped out of one of those antiques your great-aunt brings back from all over the world."

Rosie beamed happily as her mum bustled out of the room again. "So it wasn't a dream," she said to herself. "I *did* meet Azara and she *does* have a magic flying carpet. And Abdul and the palace and the peacocks – they were all *real!*"

Rosie leaned over the edge of the bed and stared down at the rug on the floor. What she saw made her gasp with delight.

The picture on the rug had changed. The lamp was no longer perched on top of the mountain peak with its lid open. Now, the lid firmly closed, it lay on the little princess's lap as she sat on her flying carpet. The picture of Azara had changed too. Instead of looking sad and forlorn, she was now smiling happily.

Rosie smiled too.

"Come on, lazybones!" said Luke, popping his head round the door with a mischievous grin. "Are you going to stay in bed all day?"

"Cheeky monster!" Rosie cried, pretending to be cross. She jumped out of bed and dashed over to the door, as Luke ran off laughing.

"I can see that life in Great-aunt Rosamund's castle is going to be very exciting!" Rosie said to herself, pulling on her dressing gown. "And I'm not going to be lonely at all. I've already made friends with one little princess, and I bet there are others. I can't wait to find the next one!"

THE END

Did you enjoy reading about Rosie's
adventure with the Whispering Princess?
If you did, you'll love the next
Little Princesses
book!

Turn over to read the first chapter of
The Fairytale Princess.

Chapter One

Rosie stood as still as she could behind the heavy velvet curtain. She could hear footsteps coming along the corridor towards her.

"Got you!" Rosie's little brother Luke pulled the curtain aside and grinned at her. "My turn to hide now."

"How did you know I was there?" Rosie laughed as they turned and walked back towards the Great Hall.

"I saw your trainers sticking out under the curtain," Luke replied. "Now, I'm going to find a really *brilliant* place to hide."

"Go on, then," Rosie said with a smile, turning away to face the roaring fire in the huge stone fireplace of the Great Hall and enjoying the heat from the orange flames. The castle could sometimes feel very cold now that it was autumn.

"Count to one hundred, Rosie, and no cheating," Luke ordered.

"What a cheek!" Rosie replied. "I *never* cheat!" She began to count. "One, two, three . . ."

Rosie heard Luke's footsteps disappear into the distance as he raced out of the Great Hall. As she counted higher, Rosie thought how lucky she and Luke were. Not many people got the chance to play hide-and-seek in a *real* castle!

"Forty-nine, fifty, fifty-one . . ."

Rosie glanced around the enormous room. Wherever she went in the castle, she was always on the lookout for little princesses. Part of the fun for Rosie was not knowing where she would find the next one.

"Eighty-eight, eighty-nine, ninety . . ." Rosie wondered where she should start looking for her brother. She glanced up at the ceiling. Maybe Luke had gone into one of the bedrooms to hide.

As she stared upwards, Rosie's gaze fell on the large tapestry that hung above the fireplace. It had been part of the Great Hall for so long, she almost didn't notice it any more. But now, a feeling of huge excitement rushed through her.

The picture showed a girl in a flowing, blue medieval gown with a gold sash around her waist. On her head was a pointed blue hat with a white veil that hung down over her long blonde hair.

To one side of the girl stood a golden dragon. He looked very fierce, with sharp

teeth and claws
and golden scales.
His mouth was
open and a stream
of orange and red
flames poured from
it. On the other
side of the girl, a
knight in shining silver armour sat,
tall and proud, on a white horse.

"She must be a little princess!" Rosie
said to herself, staring hard at the girl
in the tapestry. "She looks a bit scared.
But I'd be scared too if I was standing
right next to a dragon!"

Rosie forgot all about Luke and their
game of hide-and-seek. Remembering the
instructions in her great-aunt's letter, she took
a deep breath and bobbed down into a low

curtsey. "Hello!" she said, her eyes fixed on the girl in the blue dress.

No sooner had the word left her lips than a soft breeze rustled through the Great Hall. Rosie felt herself wrapped in a warm whirlwind that smelled faintly of summer fields and wild flowers. It lifted her gently off her feet, as Rosie closed her eyes and waited to see what would happen. Was she about to meet a little princess?

Just a moment or two later, Rosie felt her feet touch down again on soft, springy grass. The smell of summer meadows, flowers and hay was stronger now and she could feel the warmth of the sun on her skin.

Rosie opened her eyes and gasped in wonder. She was standing in the countryside on a beautiful summer's day. The scene around her was like a picture in a fairytale.

The sky overhead was
a deep blue, studded
with tiny white
clouds. All around her
were meadows dotted
with flowers, fields of

rippling golden corn and rolling green hills
stretching away in every direction.
"This is *lovely*!" Rosie sighed happily.

Then, for the first time, she noticed that
her clothes had changed too. Instead of
her jeans and sweatshirt, she was now
wearing a long, golden medieval dress
with a pointed gold hat and white veil.

Rosie smiled. She was just smoothing
down her dress and admiring her dainty
golden slippers, when she heard a strange
noise above her head.

Flap! Flap! Flap!

Rosie looked upwards, and
immediately screamed. The
golden dragon from the
tapestry was flying straight
towards her, and he
looked very real!
"Go away!" Rosie
shouted, waving her
arms. But to her
horror, the creature
opened his mouth,
ready to send
his fiery breath
shooting straight at her. The dragon was
going to burn Rosie to a crisp!

Read the rest of
The Fairytale Princess
to follow Rosie's adventures!